DOGHOUS

IN

Donkeys Don't Just Die

Also by Robin Kingsland in Red Fox

Reilly's Rules

DOGHOUSE REILLY

IN

Donkeys Don't Just Die

ROBIN KINGSLAND

RED FOX

For Fiona

A Red Fox Book

Published by Random House Children's Books
20 Vauxhall Bridge Road, London SW1V 2SA

A division of Random House UK Ltd
London Melbourne Sydney Auckland
Johannesburg and agencies throughout the world

Copyright © Robin Kingsland 1995

1 3 5 7 9 10 8 6 4 2

First published simultaneously in hardback and paperback by
The Bodley Head Children's Books and Red Fox 1995

The right of Robin Kingsland to be identified as the author of
this work has been asserted by him in accordance with the
Copyright, Designs and Patents Act, 1988

Printed and bound in Great Britain by
Cox & Wyman Ltd, Reading, Berkshire

RANDOM HOUSE UK Limited Reg. No. 954009

ISBN 0 09 911361 9

CHAPTER ONE

In this world, you're never completely in control. Life picks you up, swings you around for a while, and then puts you down again. I've been swung around a lot in my time, and I've been put down in a lot of places. All just like this one. I'd been here for three days so far — which was three days too long.

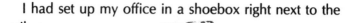

I had set up my office in a shoebox right next to the railway.

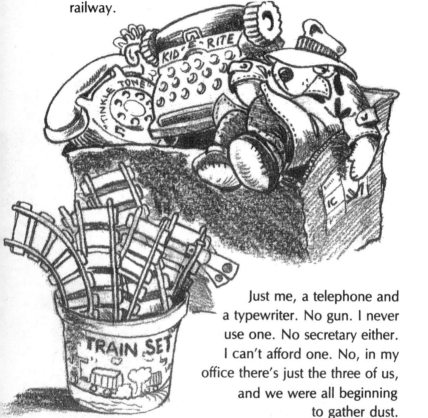

Just me, a telephone and a typewriter. No gun. I never use one. No secretary either. I can't afford one. No, in my office there's just the three of us, and we were all beginning to gather dust.

I decided to go for a walk, to clear some of the cotton wool from my head.

You've all seen places like it. In the daytime, it's a bright, colourful, happy place. A place where men, women and children laugh, and talk and play.

At night it's a different story.

At night it's all shadows and hidden places. A cluttered landscape of brick piles and discarded cars, where glittering eyes

watch you

from every

dark

corner.

I had walked enough, and I was just on my way back to the shoebox when I saw him. A little crowd had gathered around.

I didn't know it at the time, but his name was Johnny Nobody. Any other time I would have walked on by. He was a donkey like any other, and believe me, I've seen a lot of donkeys in my time.

But I'd never seen one as dead as Johnny Nobody.

CHAPTER TWO

Perhaps I should have kept my nose out. After all, asking questions is my job – I didn't want to make it a hobby too. But what the heck. It couldn't do any harm to keep in practice, could it?

I spotted one doll in the crowd. She was crying. I worked my way towards her, trying to look casual. Then I began my neat line in information gathering:

I had to give up this line of questioning. It wasn't getting me anywhere.
What it was getting me was soaked. Could that doll cry!

I was about to try plan B – the 'lend her your handkerchief and she'll tell you the whole story in her own time' technique, when I felt a tap.

Did I say a 'tap'? It felt as if someone had dropped a whole bathroom on my shoulder. I turned around, and found myself staring up into four small, mean, glittering eyes.

Luckily they were shared by two people.

It was the fat man who spoke first. When he did he sounded like rusty scissors being opened and closed.

'My name,' he wheezed, 'is Dumpty. Horatio T. Dumpty. And this is my partner, Mr Taiwan.'

'Nice to meet you,' said the gorilla, moving closer.

Charley Taiwan spoke softly too, with a voice like air escaping from something. He was even bigger than the fat man, and he looked as if he could open tins with his teeth.

'Nice' was not the word I would have used.

Dumpty had turned to the crying doll. 'Is this person upsetting you, Miss Teers?'

Miss Teers??! What kind of a name is 'Teers'?

Dumpty looked at me again. 'You ask a lot of questions, Mr er . . . '

'I've had a lot of names in my time,' I said, 'Fluffy, Fido, Phuppy-wuppy. But the name on the tag . . . ' I flashed my identification, 'Is Reilly.'

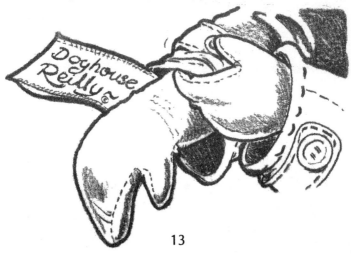

'Are you a policeman, Mr Reilly?' Dumpty asked.

'Do I look like one?' I said.

There was a pause. Charley Taiwan looked deep in thought. Maybe he was wondering what I'd look like with my ears tied in a reef knot. Maybe he was trying to remember his own name. It was kind of hard to tell.

An ambulance had picked up Johnny Nobody, and

we watched as it whirred and clanked out of sight, its feeble lights reflected in Dumpty's glinty little eyes. 'Poor Johnny,' he said.

'You knew him then?' I said. Dumpty pulled his mouth into a shape. For the sake of argument, we'll call it a smile.

'Everybody knew Johnny,' he wheezed, 'Everybody liked him.'

'Somebody didn't,' I said, and the wailing started up again.

I left the happy little group. The doll was crying harder than ever. H.T. Dumpty was comforting her. At least, he was saying, 'There, there,' and patting her shoulder. His eyes weren't comforting anybody. They were too busy boring into my back as I walked back towards the shoebox.

CHAPTER THREE

The next day, I took another walk.

I told myself it was healthy to walk. I told myself I was just strolling. I told myself I was not going to ask anybody about Johnny Nobody, or his untimely demise. I told myself it wasn't my case.

I wasn't kidding myself for a minute. It was my case, whether I liked it or not. It had been my case ever since I'd seen Johnny lying there. At that moment I had decided. *Somebody* had to find out why a donkey that 'everybody liked' had ended up so very *very* dead. And somebody, in this case, was yours truly, Doghouse Reilly. Friend of the downtrodden.

I thought I should sniff around where Johnny Nobody had lived. Perhaps his neighbours would know who he'd been seen with lately. I tracked down his address, and made my way there.

Johnny's place was in a run down part of the neighbourhood, next to a closed-off area that the locals called 'The Compound'.

The Compound was dark.

Very.

I could barely see my nose in front of my face, and mine is not the kind of nose you can easily lose. It was cold too – the place, not my nose – and silent except for a kind of hum. You could feel it under your feet, like some great machine sleeping under you. Up ahead, beyond the weird high towers, I could see light gleaming

on curves and edges of metal, and now and again there was a faint metallic hiss from the darkness. I shivered.

I tried to imagine anybody actually *living* in a neighbourhood like this, but I don't have that much imagination.

Just like me, Johnny Nobody had had a shoebox to live in, except that his was even smaller, and shabbier than mine. I knew it was Johnny's place because his name was on it, along with another one, *E. Mouse*. It was open, so I looked inside.

Nothing much. A few old clothes. Some books. A couple of music tapes. The place was not exactly brimming over with clues. I made a note; 'E. Mouse. Who's he? Find and question.' Then I left. Somebody called me. I looked around and saw a great big bear of a guy leaning against a car. 'Hey you,' he called, with a voice like crushing sugar, 'Are you Reilly?' I shouted yes, and he signalled for me to go over.

The sign behind him said **'Barney's Petrol Station.'** It had green pumps and a yellow pay booth, and it was right across from Johnny's place. I walked over. Maybe this would be my big break. Maybe this Barney had seen something.

'So, you're the private eye?' he said. News travels fast in a small place, and this was a small place.

'Well, I'm not the tooth-fairy.' I smiled. He didn't. 'What's on your mind,' I asked him.

'Last night. We went for a walk.'

'We?' I got out my notebook. I wanted to get all this down.

'Me, and the wife and kid. When we got back the place was a mess.'

'Johnny's place?'

'*Our* place. Broken chairs. Broken beds, food stolen. You just can't trust *nobody* these days.' He shook his head sadly.

I felt sorry for him, but I couldn't see where his story was leading. Finally I had to ask: 'What's this got to do with Johnny Nobody?'

He looked at me kind of sideways. 'Johnny who?'

'Johnny Nobody. The one who was found dead yesterday.'

'Nothin'.' He straightened from the car and started to bristle slightly. 'I don't know no Johnny Nobody. I just thought you might find out who stole my kid's porridge. You being a detective and all.'

I explained that I already had a case a little more serious than oat theft. He was growling as I turned away and headed home, to think.

I had to walk past Johnny's to get home. As I passed, I took one last look. And that was when I bumped into Horton.

CHAPTER FOUR

Bumped into him, did I say? I practically stepped on his head. I turned to apologise, and he didn't seem to move. I thought maybe I'd killed him, until I saw the bleary eyes open, and the wrinkled neck swivel, and there he was looking up at me.

'I'm sorry,' he said slowly, 'did I startle you?'

Startle me? That was a laugh. His fastest reflex probably took a week! I looked him over. He spoke well, with a voice like a very old, very dusty encyclopedia. Once upon a time, Horton must have really *been* someone. But somewhere along the line he had lost it all, and here he was, lying on a corner, a shell of his former self.

'I saw you outside Johnny's,' Horton said.

'You a friend of his?' I asked.

'Of course – we're old chums. I haven't seen him for a while though. How is he – d'you know?'

I broke it to him gently. 'Johnny's dead,' I said.

The old bald head wagged sadly, side to side. Then it craned back into the shadows. 'Did you hear that, Perce? Chap here says Johnny's dead.'

'Yeah?' a whining voice drawled. 'That's too bad.' Shambling out of the corner came the grubbiest penguin suit in the world. Perce looked like a waiter who'd fallen into the soup.

I didn't get home till late that evening. Instead I listened, as Horton and Perce told me a bedtime story. It seemed that once upon a time there were three people, and their names were Dumpty, and Johnny –

and Baby Teers . . .

'Johnny worked at the Club,' Perce said. 'We both did.'

'Club?' I said. 'What Club?'

'Dumpty's Club,' Horton wheezed. 'The Wendy House.'

I wrote the name in my book, then asked Perce, 'What did Johnny do? What was his job?'

'Every dirty job you could think of,' Perce said. 'Johnny washed up, set tables, ran errands. Dumpty treated him like a slave, but Johnny never complained, because Dumpty let him sing now and again.'

Sing? Johnny could sing? I must have looked surprised because Horton chimed in:

'Johnny wasn't much to look at, but he could sing like an angel. And when he and Baby Teers got together . . . magic, pure magic!'

'What sorts of music?'

'You name it.' This was Perce talking. 'Loud, soft, fast, slow. All kinds. But their special thing was love. They would sing love songs together till the band gave out. People came from all over just to listen.'

'Then,' Horton said, 'Johnny had an idea. He wanted Baby to go away with him, you know, go on the road as a singing duo. Dumpty was furious. He had a huge argument with Johnny. This was only a few days ago.'

'Did Dumpty threaten Johnny?' I asked.

Perce and Horton looked at each other. They didn't know. 'We weren't there, you see. We heard all this from Ricci.'

I must have looked blank, because Perce carried on, 'Ricci. Enrico Mouse. Johnny's best friend.'

Of course. E. Mouse. How did he fit into all this?

The Mouse, it seems, had ambition. As Horton put it, 'That kid had dreams like I have wrinkles!' More than anything in the world, Ricci wanted to be in show business. Not just any show business, either. For The Mouse, it was going to be The Movies, or nothing.

Frankly, most people in the neighbourhood thought 'Nothing'.

'You'd understand if you met Ricci,' Perce said. 'Great personality, heart of gold – but he had this weird little high-pitched voice, and the biggest ears you've seen this side of an elephant. You could pick up Moscow radio on those wingnuts. Johnny and I tried to put him off the movies idea – we didn't want him to be disappointed – but Ricci stuck to his plan. Some day, he kept saying, he was going to change his name to Micki, and take the movies by storm. That poor mixed-up mouse. I think it was him gave Johnny the idea of going on the road with Baby Teers.'

'Do you know where Enrico is now?' I said. That was one mouse I'd like to talk to. Horton and Perce shook their heads.

Then Perce said, 'Come to think of it, I haven't seen *him* for a few days either! You don't suppose . . .'

Great! First there was Johnny, now some mouse had disappeared. Things were going from bad to worse, and I'd only been on the case a day.

CHAPTER FIVE

Baby Teers and Johnny. Johnny and Dumpty. Dumpty and Baby Teers. Little pieces of this jigsaw were starting to fit into place. Dumpty was mean, powerful and used to getting his own way. He was jealous of Johnny and Baby Teers singing together. Insanely jealous. So, he killed Johnny. Or had him killed. Of course, it all made sense. I had my case. I had my killer. All I needed now was some hard evidence. It was time to go and see Mr H.T. Dumpty at his club.

I was just heading home to put on a clean tie, when something shot out of the shadows behind me.

I ran. I ran as fast as I could. I didn't dare look behind me. Whoever, *whatever* it was, I didn't want to see it.

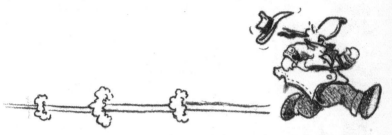

It was enough to hear the sound it made as it gained on me. It sounded like the whizzing of a demented dentist's drill. I tried swerving. Wherever I swerved it swerved too.

I could imagine its razor-sharp teeth. I ran harder. I skidded round a corner, collided with some bins and went bowling over with a tremendous clatter. And then it was on me.

CHAPTER SIX

Yip! Yip! Yip!
Yip!
Yip! Yip! Yip! Yip!
Yip!
Yip! Yip! Yip!
Yip! Yip!
Yip!
Yip!
Yip! Yip!
Yip!
Yip! Yip! Yip!
Yip!

CHAPTER SEVEN

There are many things I don't know, but I'll tell you one thing I *do* know. I know this: 'Yip yip yip yip,' is not the sound of horrible, razor-toothed death. I levered myself up from the tumble of bins, and got a squint at what had been following me.

It was small, and it was furry, and it was about as threatening as a pyjama case. I looked around. I was back on familiar territory, but there wasn't another soul in sight. Good. If anyone got to hear about *this*, my reputation as a hard-boiled private eye would be in shreds. I could hear the gossip already . . . 'He *ran?* from a little *fur-ball?* You don't say!'

The little fur-ball in question was still there. 'Yip yip yip yip yip,' it went, and whizzed around on the spot for a couple of seconds, like a mad thing. I stood up.

'You want to play, huh?' I said, grumpily. 'Well, I don't!' I dusted myself off, and started to walk.

Whizzzzzzz.

It was following me. I stopped and turned. 'I'd throw you a stick,' I snapped, 'but I'm all out of dynamite. So go away!'

It didn't move. It just sat there, looking as if it intended to stay on the spot until doomsday, and never yip or whizz for another living soul. A sadder pile of fur you never saw.

'What's the matter with you!?' I yelled. 'Get out of here! Vamoose! Go back wherever you came from before I call a cop! *SCRAM!*' The fur-ball yelped and scooted back the way it had come, zig-zagging from side to side as it went.

I walked on, and thought about tomorrow. Tomorrow was a big day. Tomorrow I was going to talk to the people's friend, Mr Horatio Dumpty.

CHAPTER EIGHT

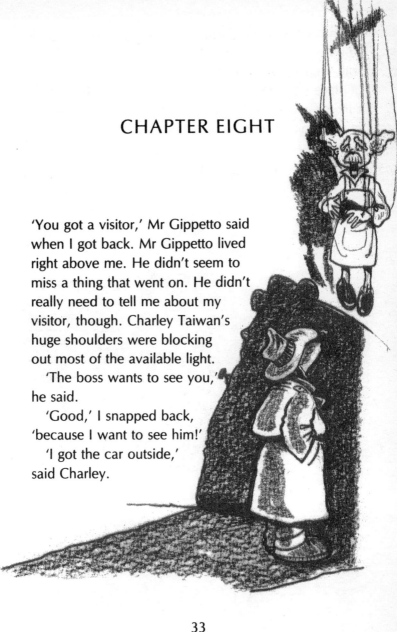

'You got a visitor,' Mr Gippetto said
when I got back. Mr Gippetto lived
right above me. He didn't seem to
miss a thing that went on. He didn't
really need to tell me about my
visitor, though. Charley Taiwan's
huge shoulders were blocking
out most of the available light.

'The boss wants to see you,'
he said.

'Good,' I snapped back,
'because I want to see him!'

'I got the car outside,'
said Charley.

Dumpty's Club was a surprise. I had expected it to be a gloomy, smoky dive, but it wasn't. It was big and airy, with arches, and pillars and pretty pictures – the kind of place you could take your grandmother. There was a little band playing. Just drums and the tank-tinky-tonk of a tiny piano, but the music was good.

Dumpty was sitting in a corner, surrounded by what looked like a small army.

'Who's this?' I said, 'All the King's horses and all the King's men?'

'I was just about to have tea, Mr Reilly,' Dumpty wheezed. 'Would you care to join me?'

'I don't drink with killers!' I said.

The big man smiled. Well, he showed his teeth anyway. 'I'm a businessman, Mr Reilly,' he said quietly, 'I don't kill people.'

'Maybe not, Dumpty,' I looked up at Charley Taiwan, 'But maybe you give the orders to the kind of gorilla that does! And that's the same thing in my book.'   .

The band had stopped playing. Everyone in the place was watching and listening. Dumpty smiled again. This one you could have built igloos with. 'We should talk in private,' he said. 'Follow me.' It was more like an order than an invitation. I looked up at Charley again and he gave me a prod. I followed Dumpty.

We walked out back. As soon as we were alone, Dumpty turned on me. 'I don't like your attitude, Mr Detective,' he growled.

'I've got a nicer one,' I cracked, 'but it's away at the cleaners.'

'What makes you think that I had anything to do with Johnny's death?'

I told him what I'd found out. All about him and Baby Teers, and Johnny, and how Dumpty was jealous of them, and how he'd argued with Johnny. Dumpty sat back in a big chair and heard me out. When I'd finished, he got up and walked around me, looking at me like I was something the cat dragged in and might drag out again any second.

'You amaze me, Mr Reilly. You really do. You've been here – how long . . . a few days? – and already you think you know it all. Let me tell you something – '

He stopped. Back in the club, the tonky-tank piano had started up again. We both looked through the curtain as Miss Baby Teers began to sing.

She sang about broken hearts and lost love, and there wasn't a dry eye in the place, including hers. She could sing, sure, but Baby Teers was up there doing what she did best –

she was crying her eyes out.

When she finished singing, the place went crazy. I'd almost forgotten about Dumpty, until he spoke right behind me: 'Of *course* I didn't want her to go with Johnny. Without her this club would be nothing. Listen to that crowd. They love her.

Do you think I'd let a jumped up bottle-washer like Johnny Nobody take her off to the bright lights? Of course not! I told him so. If that's what you call an argument, we had an argument.'

'Is that when you decided to have him killed?'

Dumpty looked at me for a long time without speaking. Then he said, 'Mr Taiwan will show you out, Reilly.'

Charley appeared in the door. He'd show me out alright – on my feet, my head or my butt-end, he didn't seem particular about which. I turned to go. Then, on a wild impulse, I said casually, 'Do you know a character called Enrico?'

'That's none of your – ' Dumpty began, but Charley Taiwan, big on bulk, low on brain, helped me out.

Dumpty gave the gorilla a look you could chill fish on. Then he turned back to me with a paper-thin smile.

'Now I come to think of it,' he said softly, 'I *do* know the gentleman.'

'Did you know he's missing?' I said.

Now, either Dumpty was a brilliant actor, or he didn't know about Ricci's disappearance. If only I could work out which it was.

'Ricci's gone walkies, and Johnny's come down with a nasty case of dead . . . and *you* knew both of them. That makes you my chief suspect. Chew on that, Dumpty.'

CHAPTER NINE

I got back to the shoebox. It was late, I was tired, and I guessed no one else would be up. I guessed wrong. Mr Gippetto was always up.

'Hi Mr Gippetto,' I called up. 'How's your boy?'

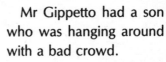

Mr Gippetto had a son who was hanging around with a bad crowd.

'Ach,' the old man pulled a hopeless face, 'I don't know *vat* to do with him, Mr Reilly,' he sighed, 'I tell him, "Pinocchio, vye don't you *make* something of yourself?!"'

I looked up. 'What did he say to that?'

'He say "Vot you *va*nt I should make of myself? A deck chair, maybe?" Pffff! Kids!' He turned away slowly, then turned back again. 'By de vey, Mr Reilly, someone vos in your place tonight.'

I froze.

'Who?' I said. Mr Gippetto shrugged. 'I'm an old man. My eyes don't see so good. I just hear them come in and go out.'

I shuffled into the shoebox. Mr Gippetto was right. Someone *had* been there. Things had been moved. My telephone was on the floor. And there was a note in the typewriter:

CHAPTER TEN

E. Mouse? So, Ricci was still in circulation. That was something anyway.

I sat and stared at the note for a while. How did Enrico know where to find me? It was curious. Call me suspicious if you like, but a light kept flashing in my head with '**TRAP**' written on it in foot-high letters. *Come alone.* MacDonald's farm was quiet and out of the way. Just the place for an ambush. But in the end I knew I had to go, trap or no trap. I had to go because it was the only lead I had.

I clambered into my car, turned the key, and headed out to the farm.

MacDonald's Farm was run down. Old MacDonald had retired so now it was Young MacDonald's Farm, which didn't have the same ring to it. The sign was broken and so were most of the fences.

I drove the car through the entrance and took my feet off the pedals. I listened to the silence that sat like a mist over the whole place.

Then I
got out of the car
and walked towards
the nearest barn.

The roof was caved in, and the door lay on the ground a good way from the hole it was supposed to fill. It may have been my imagination, but it looked as if it had only been broken off recently. I stepped inside.

It was a mess, even by MacDonald's Farm standards.

There had obviously been a Grandaddy of a struggle here. Stacks of barrels had been sprawled across the floor, and there were churnings of what looked like tank tracks everywhere. Maybe Young MacDonald rented his farm out for army manoeuvres. But I didn't think so. Something winked at me from the floor. I stopped and picked it up. It was a button. It looked familiar too. I'd seen three more just like it – on Dumpty's waistcoat.

I heard a sound like a snapping twig out by the gate. 'Mr Mouse?' I called softly. 'Enrico? It's me, Reilly.' Next second I froze. All the hairs on the back of my

46

neck stood to attention as a high-pitched screech sliced through the air. It lasted for two seconds, maybe three. Then a silence so heavy it thumped as it came down.

I was out of the door and heading for the gate at a fast clip when something as heavy as the silence hit the back of my head.

I was right. It was a heck of a good place for an ambush.

CHAPTER ELEVEN

I woke up cold, feeling
as if I'd been unravelled.

My car had been flattened like a paper cup. I had to
walk home. By the time I got back to the shoebox I was
mad. Mad enough to go to Dumpty's. When I reached
the Wendy House I marched past Charley Taiwan. He
was too surprised to even try to stop me.

I walked straight up to Dumpty. 'Ever been to
MacDonald's Farm?' I asked. He looked genuinely
surprised. No, he said, he hadn't ever been there.

The secret of Crimebusting is patience. No matter
how clever a criminal is, sooner or later they'll make
a mistake. They'll say something, or do something,

some tiny little thing, that gives them away, and then WAMMO! you slap on the cuffs and it's 'Good night and thank you!'

I whipped the button out of my pocket, held it up, and sneered,

'Well if you've never been to MacDonald's Farm, how come I found *this* there! Answer that!'

Dumpty didn't crumble to dust when he saw the button. He didn't run, either, and he showed no sign of dropping to his knees and confessing his horrible crime. Instead he just said, 'It's the wrong size.'

I stared at the button. Then at Dumpty. Then at Dumpty's waistcoat button again. He was right. The one I had found was the same colour as those on Dumpty's waistcoat, and the same design. Just slightly smaller. I looked around. One or two of the customers were giggling. Charley Taiwan had finally pulled himself together. He came lumbering over.

'You want me to bounce this guy, boss?' he said.

'That won't be necessary, Mr Taiwan, our friend was just leaving, weren't you, Mr Reilly.'

I wondered if anything was going to make this guy crack? I had to rattle him, make him mad. Then maybe he would let slip some clue. I went to leave. Then, at the last moment, I turned and said:

'I'm sorry I bothered you. I think you killed Johnny, and I think you've killed Enrico mouse, but I've got no

proof, so it looks as if you'll get away with it, doesn't it
. . . Humpty.'

He cracked all right. Spluttering with rage he bundled
over towards me with Charley Taiwan right behind him.
The gorilla was all over me in seconds.

'My name is *Horatio*!!' Dumpty hissed, 'NOBODY
calls me . . . what you just called me!'

'Don't get so excited,' I said. 'It's bad for your
blood-pressure. Is this how mad you were when you
bumped off Johnny?'

Dumpty backed off, and straightened his bow tie. His beady eyes bore into me, and he spoke as quietly as a bomb ticking. 'For the last time, Reilly, I did not "bump off" Johnny or anyone else. It's not my style. We had a difference of opinion over Miss Teers . . . on the evening he died, I admit that . . . but by the time he left he'd calmed down.'

I sneered. 'Sure Dumpty. It's the oldest story in the book. "He was just *fine* when he left here, officer!" And I suppose you've no idea where he went after that?'

'As a matter of fact I do,' said Dumpty. 'I sent him on an errand.'

'Going to tell me where you sent him?' I asked.

'I'll do better than that, Mr Reilly. I'll *take* you there. Charley, fetch the car.'

CHAPTER TWELVE

Charley drove. Charley Taiwan, the man of a million jobs. Driver, doorman, bodyguard . . . not bad for an airhead. I wondered if he was Dumpty's muscleman too. I wondered if he was going to enjoy tearing me apart, because that was surely the purpose of the drive.

The car glided to a stop in a deserted street. We got out.

'Hey,' I said. 'I know this place. This is – '

'The Compound.' Dumpty said. 'It was on his way home, so Johnny said he would take a message for me that night.'

I peered into the Compound. The smell of oil wafted from it. 'Johnny went in there?' I said, alarmed. 'At night? *Alone*? Who did he come to see?'

'Them!' said Dumpty, and there was a deep loathing in his beady eyes. 'The robots!'

'Robots?' I said. This was starting to sound a little crazy. Dumpty explained.

'The Compound wasn't always here,' he said, 'it all started when the first robots came. They seemed 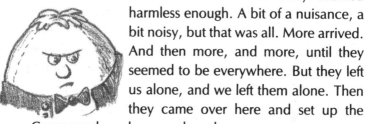 harmless enough. A bit of a nuisance, a bit noisy, but that was all. More arrived. And then more, and more, until they seemed to be everywhere. But they left us alone, and we left them alone. Then they came over here and set up the Compound, and no-one heard or saw them again.' Dumpty fell silent.

'Until? . . .' I prompted.

'Until a few days ago. They came back. But this time they were different. They started pushing the rest of us around, telling us where we could go. They started barking about 'restricted zones', like they were the cops or something! I mean they're not even real. They've got nothing inside but wires and cogs and serial numbers. It's like being told what to do by a parking meter!

They even started hanging around outside the club. They were putting off my customers. That's why I sent Johnny over here. To give their boss a message to stay away from my club!'

Dumpty carried on talking, but I didn't hear what he said. The pieces of this giant jigsaw were starting to fit together. I didn't have all the pieces yet, but the ones I had were finally making sense to me. I was trying to figure where Enrico the Mouse fitted into things when Dumpty nudged me in the ribs.

'Come on,' he said, 'Let's get out of here. This place gives me the creeps!'

We clambered into the car and swung away from the shadows of the Compound.

CHAPTER THIRTEEN

I didn't say a word all the way back. I was too busy thinking. Thinking about Johnny and robots. Robots and Dumpty. Dumpty and Baby Teers. Baby Teers and Johnny. Suddenly I turned to Dumpty.

'Turn around,' I said. 'I'm going to talk to them.'

'Who?'

'The robots.'

Dumpty turned pale. 'Are you out of your mind!? They're *machines*. You can't talk to a machine! Even if you could get into that Compound you'd probably be zapped or something. I tell you –'

He never did tell me, because at that moment, something huge loomed up in front of us. It was like a vast bubble-gum machine on legs, big as a building and shiny as a car 'LOOK OUT, CHARLEY!' Dumpty screeched.

Charley Taiwan heaved at the steering wheel, but it was too late;

there was a yowl of brakes, a tearing screeching metallic sound, the world flipped through three quick somersaults, and everything went black.

CHAPTER FOURTEEN

'Mr Reilly . . . ? Mr Reilly . . . ?'

I was lying on the ground. Out of the corner of my eye, I could still see the wheels of Dumpty's car turning stupidly, clickety clickety clickety click. The car had looked expensive. Now it just looked short.

'Mr Reilly? Are you OK?'

I looked up – to see a pair of familiar eyes. Miss Baby Teers was kneeling beside me, bandaging my arm.

'Dumpty?' I said, 'Is he . . . ' I didn't want to say the word. It was the first time I had seen her and not had her cry all over me. I wanted to keep it that way if I could. Miss Teers shook her head.

'He and Mr Taiwan managed to roll clear of the car,' she said.

'I imagine our friend Dumpty rolls pretty well,' I said.

'Don't be too hard on him,' Miss Teers said. 'He may have his faults, but he's a fine, fine person in many ways.'

I seemed to have forgotten how to stand up without

leaning over. I touched a tender spot on my nose. 'It needs some attention,' Miss Teers said, and held up a first-aid kit.

I tried to talk without moving my nose too much. I told her I'd heard about her and Johnny, and she told me that Johnny really had been fine that night when he left the Wendy House. 'Mr Dumpty likes to play tough,' she said, 'but deep down he liked Johnny. He would never have hurt him.'

'Then who – ow! – who did?' She shrugged, and tied off the last stitch. 'I just don't know Mr Reilly. Ricci. . . Enrico. . . he told me that he had some information. I told him to come to you. Did he?'

Another piece of the jigsaw slotted into place. Baby Teers had sent Ricci the Mouse to me. I wondered how I was going to tell her he was missing, but I was saved the trouble, because at that moment we heard a groan and Dumpty and Charley shuffled over.

Dumpty looked shaken but not scrambled. Charley looked much worse. Maybe the accident had let some of the air out of his head?

'That thing we hit,' I said, 'I guess that was a robot?'

'Sure it was,' Dumpty fumed. 'A Transmixer, or a Metalloid, or something. They all have such stupid names!'

'I don't suppose you got his registration number?' I drawled. Dumpty just glared at me.

'I'm telling you, Reilly,' he snapped, 'they are taking over. Soon there will only be Metalloids and Transfixers and HY-Bots and Robonoids. You mark my words it'll happen, if we let it.'

'Go home and get that head seen to,' I said. 'You may have a crack in there somewhere.'

'What about you?'

I wondered if he was concerned, or just suspicious. 'I'm going home,' I said, 'to finish a jigsaw.'

I got home, fell into the shoebox and slept.

CHAPTER FIFTEEN

I woke up thinking. I carried on thinking all day, putting the picture together piece by piece. I kept at it until I felt my brain start to fry, but in the end I knew I had the case cracked. There was only one piece of the jigsaw missing.

And to get it, I had to go back to the Compound.

I had to walk all the way and it was dark when I reached the gates. One thing was for sure. The place didn't get friendlier. It still had all the appeal of a barbed wire vest.

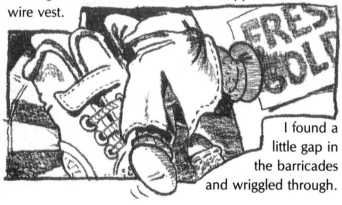

I found a little gap in the barricades and wriggled through.

It was eerie. Out of the dark, a few feeble lights blinked. Some were just a sickly glimmer in the murk, some rose and fell in scales of light, as if their batteries were breathing. Here and there were panels which emitted rippling waves of blue, green and red. All shrugged their watery alien light on to the jungle of plastic limbs, as the air pulsed with purrs, clicks and hums. If an amusement arcade had married a junkyard, and they had had a child, I guess it would have looked like this place.

I could see Dumpty's point about these characters. If they were this scary to be around when they were 'sleeping', what would they be like 'awake'?

I didn't have to wait long to find out.

The voice sounded like a wasp in a tin bucket. I thought about running, but I'd already come too far in. I was surrounded, and I quickly saw when every bit of 'floor' around me seemed to erupt and lift and snap and click and slide and grow, and grow some more. I hate this! I thought to myself, as something big rattled up on tank tracks, cutting off any chance I might have had of a quick getaway.

'IDENTIFY!' It was Bucket Voice again. 'IDENTIFY INTRUDER!'

Tanktrax played a little red light beam into my ear, fluttered a few ariels, and announced, 'Soft intruder. No Power source.'

'HOLD INTRUDER.'

The robots began to edge even closer.

'Er, hello!' I yelled, hoping that Bucket Voice – wherever he was – could hear me. 'Could we *discuss* this? I come in peace... er ... take me to your leader!'

It was a stupid thing to say, because that was where they were *going* to take me, whether I liked it or not.

CHAPTER SIXTEEN

I couldn't see much of the leader at first. All I could see, in fact, were two glowing eyes of a kind that managed to be red and cold at the same time, and the occasional glimmer of polished armour plating.

I have to confess something. I don't like my office, the shoebox. It is dusty and cramped and uncomfortable, and there is never enough light. But right at the moment, I wanted to be there, or in a sewer, or buried up to my neck in snakes. I wanted to be anywhere but where I was.

The thing with the red eyes growled. I thought this would be Bucket Voice, but it wasn't. This one wasn't as *friendly* as Bucket Voice. This one said, 'You are one of the soft ones.'

'I beg your pardon,' I said. That's me. Always polite, even to dangerous-sounding robots. Come to think of it, *especially* to dangerous-sounding robots.

The growler lumbered nearer. Oh, boy, was he BIG! I could see the name on his chest now.

Hy-Tek

it said.

'Soft ones are not permitted in this sector!' he barked.

'Soft ones?'

Hy-Tek's arm swung in a tight arc, and slammed against his own armoured chest. 'Hard!' he explained. His arm began to rise above me. He was going to demonstrate who he meant by soft.

'I get the idea!' I said quickly, and the arm lowered with a whirr, and came to rest with a click.

'The environment here cannot support two life forms,' said Hy-Tek in an almost reasonable tone. 'The weaker must give way.' I tipped back my hat and chuckled. 'Something is funny?' he rasped.

'They used to say, "This town ain't big enough for both of us,"' I said. 'It amounts to the same thing. The bully boys pushing everyone else out!'

'It is the survival of the fittest!' the robot snapped. 'Look at you. You are threadbare, overweight, you have no power. We are precision made, powered by fail-safe motors. We have guaranteed survival. We are indestructible!'

'You've been reading your own manual, buddy!' I said.

Hy-Tek's eyes blazed brighter. 'You disappoint me,' he said. 'We had hoped to avoid the use of physical force!' He looked to me like the sort of character who was *itching* to use physical force, but I kept that opinion to myself. Tanktrax was right behind me, and ready to roll me into dog food if I spoke out of turn.

Hy-Tek was still talking:

'We had hoped that the soft ones would move aside

71

to make way for us. But you are a stubborn people, and you leave us no alternative. We must drive you out, or destroy you!'

This was a crazy robot.

'Drive us out?' I shouted. 'Just like *that*??'

No. Not just like that. Apparently, they had been working for weeks, laying plans for a complete takeover. A mass attack had been prepared. The metal heads versus the 'soft ones'. One night to finish it once and for all. To decide who would be the masters.

One night.

This night.

I should have been frightened. I should have been wondering how to warn the other 'soft ones' before it was too late. But a detective has his pride. I was sure now that I knew what had happened to the Donkey, but I had to *know*. I had to *know* that I was right. I looked up into those cold red eyes.

'Hey. Did you ever come across Johnny Nobody?' I asked.

Hy-Tek wheeled round to Tanktrax. 'Compute!' he ordered.

Tanktrak's lights went into overdrive, and a dull whirring came from somewhere around where his navel should have been.

'Nobody. First name, Johnny,' he whined. 'Soft species, intruded on planning council.

So. I *was* right. The last piece of the jigsaw fell into place. Dumpty had sent Johnny to talk to these . . . things. He'd arrived slap-bang in the middle of their pow-wow. The wrong donkey in the wrong place at the wrong time. Funny how these things turn out. Johnny Nobody was the last person you'd suspect of knowing too much. About anything!

I took my hat off to Hy-Tek. 'Well, it's been nice meeting you,' I said, 'but I left the toaster on.' I tried to slide back and sideways. 'You must meet my toaster some day, you have so much in common . . . !'

'HOLD HIM!' Hy-Tek barked.

I tried to make a break for it, but it was hopeless, really. I was hemmed in by machines. Imagine you're in a discount electrical shop, and you know that if you move, every fridge, washing machine and microwave will jump on you. Then you'll have some idea how I felt. I decided to go along quietly for the time being. I make a good detective – I'd make a lousy pancake!

Hy-Tek lumbered towards me. 'I am truly sorry to say this,' he began to say, but I already knew the routine. I couldn't imitate the metallic grind of his voice, but I had a darned good try:

'I know. You're truly sorry to say this, but now I know too much and cannot be allowed to go free. Am I close?'

The big metal face bent close to mine. The red eyes blazed.

'I couldn't have put it better myself,' he said.

74

Ten minutes later I was still breathing. That was the good news. The bad news was that I was in a glass tank, in a box, in the dark. 'Well,' I said to myself, 'you're really in trouble now!'

I jumped out of my skin at the freaky, high-pitched voice that answered.

'Er, I'm sorry,' the mouse said. 'Were you speaking to me?'

CHAPTER SEVENTEEN

Horton had been right about Ricci the mouse. He looked weird, and he sounded weirder. If his voice had been any higher he could have got a job as a kettle whistle!

'Hey, you're the detective,' he squeaked. 'Miss Teers told me about you. I sent you a note. So, the robots got you too, huh?'

I shrugged. 'Looks that way.'

We got talking – there wasn't much else to do – and Ricci filled in the few tiny gaps left in my theory of the Johnny Nobody case. Johnny had gone home before going to the Compound, and Ricci, being a good pal, had refused to let the donkey go alone. He'd seen the robots carry Johnny's body from the Compound and leave it where it was found. Of course he'd been terrified. He'd gone into hiding at MacDonalds.

'That's where Miss Teers found me, and told me to see you,' he said. 'I left you the note. But the robots must have followed me back to the farm.' Of course. The tracks on the barn floor. Tanktrax must have got him.

76

'What do you think they'll do to us?' he asked.

I decided not to tell him. I shuddered to think how high that voice would go if Ricci panicked. In this confined space he'd probably blow my ears off! I sat in a corner and thought for a long time. I didn't even notice that Ricci was speaking until he said,

'What did you think?'

'Huh?'

'What did you think?'

I must have looked totally blank, because his face fell about a hundred feet, 'of my acting pieces. I just did them for you.'

I made the best of it. 'Oh, *them*! I thought you were asking about something else. No, really, Ricci, your acting pieces were . . . uh . . . fabulous. Brilliant. I think you have a great future.'

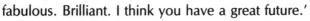

Well, what would *you* have said? Listen, in a couple of hours' time, when their attack was over, those metal psychos were going to come back, and then poor little star-struck Ricci was going to be turned into chutney with ears. So what harm did it do to tell him, just once, what he wanted to hear?

77

The mouse was wearing a wall-to-wall grin. 'You're the first person who's ever said that to me,' he beamed. He paced, trying to think of a way of showing his appreciation for my belief in him. Finding one, he wheeled round suddenly, flung his arms wide and said, 'You wanna hear me sing?'

Tact was called for here. A gentle letting down.

'No!' I said. It wasn't that I thought his voice would be bad – just high. Even if I only had a couple of hours to live, I wanted to keep my eardrums for the duration. I saw Ricci's face fall again, and he shambled back into a corner. I felt terrible for upsetting him, but his singing would have been enough to . . .

Enough to shatter glass!

'Er, Ricci,' I said, in my most encouraging voice, 'exactly how high can that voice of yours go?'

I was glad I hadn't had my coat washed. I found a couple of bits of old cotton fluff to block my ears with as Ricci sailed piercingly up and down the scales. Every time he looked at me I waved my hand, mouthing the word 'Higher?' The air seemed to be shaking and shivering into liquid slices. My ears began to hurt. Cotton fluff was no protection against Ricci. Another notch up the scale, and even he began to look pained. His ears started to ripple and pulsate as sound waves crashed together in the confined space.

'I think you're close!' I screamed, 'Can you get

any higher?'

Ricci gasped for breath, and clutched his throat. 'I don't think so, Mr Reilly.'

'Try!'

Ricci summoned all his reserves of energy. He jackknifed back, filling his lungs and throwing his head back till you could barely see his nose over his chest. Then he let fly.

It was the
sound of a
fingernail
on a
blackboard,
only
twelve
hundred
times
more so!
Ricci
held
the note,
slowly uncoiling
and then
doubling
forward
as he put
his last
blip of
energy
into
it.

Something caught my eye. I looked round and saw the snaking, shivering lines of cracks leap up the glass walls.

'That's it, Ricci,' I yelled. 'You've cracked it!'
'With one last, ear-shattering screech, Ricci collapsed gasping. There was a pause, as we heard radiating splits chasing themselves through the fabric of our cell. Then,

with a deep KA-POW! and a glittering shower of broken glass, the walls seemed to fold themselves into delicate patterns, layer on falling layer. Covering our heads, Ricci and I waited for stillness to set in.

'Did I do alright, Mr. Reilly? Did I, huh?'

'Ricci,' I said, slapping him on the back, 'You did great.'

'Just great!'

CHAPTER EIGHTEEN

We raced back towards the club, picking our way through piles of spilled bricks. I could hear a distant rumble from the direction of the Compound. The metalloids were on the move. As we neared the Wendy House I told Ricci about Hy-Tek's plan. 'Oh, my Gosh!' was all he said.

'If we hurry,' I yelled over my shoulder, 'we can warn the others before the attack starts!'

The usual crowds
were sitting in cars,
standing on corners,
ignorant of the danger
they were in, unaware
that they were about to have
the stuffing knocked out
of them by armour-plated
power-crazed jumped-up
kitchen appliances.
I couldn't tell them.
They'd just assume
I was nuts. I needed
someone to tell them
for me, to organise defences.
Someone with influence.
Someone they'd all listen to.

Someone like Horatio T. Dumpty.

I found him in the back of his Wendy House, talking to Miss Teers and another doll, whose name I didn't catch. Lindy? Bimby? I didn't have time to worry. I told Dumpty the story. Every time I paused for breath, Ricci would tug Dumpty's sleeve, and nod furiously, and gibber, 'It's true, Mr Dumpty, sir. Every word. Uhuh, it's true alright!'. In the end Charley Taiwan had to pick him up and put him in a corner and turn a syphon on him to make him calm down.

'Mr Taiwan,' Dumpty wheezed, when I'd finished, 'please bring the telephone. I must make some calls.'

I'd gone to the right guy. Ten minutes later the word was out. Nobody questioned what they were told. It came from H.T. Dumpty. That was all anybody needed to know.

CHAPTER NINETEEN

Makeshift barricades were thrown together out of anything we could lay our hands on.

Dumpty surprised everyone – he was the first to throw off his coat and start hauling blocks. Even Horton was impressed. 'I never thought I'd say it,' he announced in his plummy drawl, 'but underneath it all, Dumpty's a good egg.'

The minutes ticked by, and still there was no sign of the Metalloids. After the mad rush to prepare the defences, the helpless waiting was driving us all nuts.

'Why don't they come?' Said Miss Baby Teers.

'Maybe they changed their minds boss.' It was Charley Taiwan. Dumpty and Baby and I looked at the big ape in disbelief. Charley was embarrassed. 'Well, it's possible, ain't it?' he mumbled.

More time passed, and the silence deepened. Dumpty looked across at me. 'Scared?' he said.

'What?' I snorted, 'Me? Scared? Hey, I'm a private eye. I work with danger. Risk is my business. Hah? Me scared? Never!' I laughed a hearty laugh.

Dumpty looked me square in the eye. 'Terrified, huh? Me too!'

'I was all wrong about you, wasn't I, Dumpty?' I said.

'Forget it,' Dumpty waved his hand, 'I was wrong about you too, but it's all in the past now. We've both got other things to worry about.'

As he spoke, word came that lights had been seen in the Compound.

'Oh, boy!' Ricci said, 'Oh, my *gosh*!'

'This is it,' Dumpty said. He turned to Charley, 'Good luck, my friend.'

Charley drew himself up so straight, his knuckles nearly left the ground. 'I won't let you down boss.'

They came in a blaze of light. Tall ones, short ones; wide, squat, black, grey, red and green. I could see Hy-Tek at the head of them.

They rumbled, and hissed and ground and hummed towards us, until they seemed to fill the horizon. Closer, they came closer and closer and closer . . . and then . . .

'Chaaaaaaaaaaaaaaaaaarge!' Dumpty yelled.

If it's possible for a robot to be surprised, we took 'em by surprise. We threw everything we had at them. Including ourselves. The ponies from the *Kyooty Hooves* Stable went down in the first wave. They were foolhardy, but they were fearless too; their long, impractical manes flying as they charged.

By the time they came back they looked like retired
pit-ponies, and the robots hadn't even slowed down.

Then it was the soldiers'
turn. They tried hard too,
but were forced back by
sheer weight of machinery.
And still the robots came.

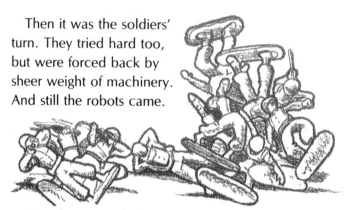

Hy-Tek's voice barked across the battlefield: 'Give yourselves up. Your puny efforts at resistance can have no effect!'

'Oh yeah,' Dumpty sneered. 'You ain't seen nothing yet! Isn't that right, Miss Teers . . .'

He looked. Miss Teers had gone. Disappeared. I hadn't seen her go, neither had Charley Taiwan. Dumpty's face went through the whole range from frightened to angry and back again. 'Miss Teers!' he shouted above the clash of battle.

Miss Teers! Where are you?

Suddenly Ricci Mouse piped up, 'There she is, Mr Dumpty. Oh, my gosh! – she's heading straight for them!'

It was true. Baby Teers had climbed the barricade, and was walking, unarmed, head high, straight into the thick of things. Like magic, the noise stopped. A calm descended. Everybody was watching Baby Teers. She was standing in front of Tanktrax. Suddenly her voice rang out:

'You killed Johnny, didn't you?' she said, 'You and your robot cronies.' Tears began to well up in her eyes. 'We could have been big stars, me and Johnny, we could have made it, if you hadn'a . . . hadn'a KILLED him. I – I – I HATE YOOOOOOOOOO!'

And then the waterworks started. You'd think a fire hydrant had burst or something. Baby Teers collapsed sobbing on to Tanktrax.

The effect on the robot was weird. His low growl disappeared, to be replaced by a high-pitched squeal of pure panic. He slammed into reverse, almost losing his balance. Still Baby Teers clung on, ignoring his struggles, crying fit to bust. 'Release! Release!' the robot squealed.

'What's happening?' Dumpty asked. 'Why is he trying to get away?'

'Maybe he's scared of water.' Charley said.

It was the first smart thing he'd said in his life. Of course. Of *course*! The robots were electrical. Their whole being depended on keeping their circuits dry. And cogs rust too. They'd seize up if they got wet!

'Where can we get water?' I yelled to Dumpty . . .

'There's a fire engine somewhere!' he said, and the word was passed down –

Tanktrax was in trouble now.

Blue electrical flashes were starting to explode around his head. His smooth whirs and clicks were turning into grinding squeals and metallic pops, as he tried to get away from Baby Teers. His wheels screamed like a car stuck in wet mud.

Then suddenly he seemed to jerk bolt upright.

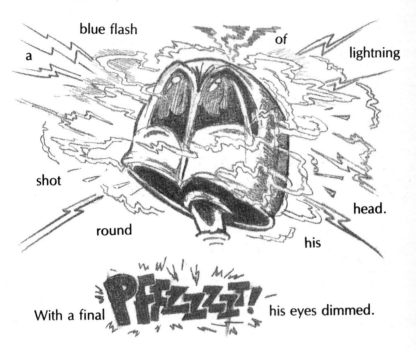

blue flash of lightning a shot round his head.

With a final PFFZZZT! his eyes dimmed.

Tanktrax was out of the fight.

Run, Miss Teers – RUN!

The fire engine had arrived. Charley and I pulled the fire hose round. Ricci was on the handle. Dumpty yelled 'Fire!' and we let them have it. Just as Baby Teers scrambled over the barricade. As the water fell into their ranks, the Metalloids began to panic. Wheeling round in a desperate attempt to avoid terminal damp they began to collide. Some of them simply fell over each other. Others, armed with zappers and lasers, began to fire without apparently caring what they hit. Mostly they hit each other.

Talk about fireworks. It was Guy Fawkes and the Fourth of July all rolled into one with the Queen's birthday thrown in.

We had to cover our eyes against the glare. We could still see flashes. Cascades of brilliant blue-white sparks and drifting fingers of acrid smoke began to thread through the air. Robots fell, crashing like dominoes, going down in twos and threes, then in waves.

Soon the great invading army was a pile of smoking junk. Only Hy-Tek stood defiant amid the shattered remains of his robot force. We saw each other at the same moment. His red eyes glared at me as he slammed his fist against his chest and roared 'HARD!!' Then he slowly raised his twin laser-cannon arms. Those eyes pinned me where I stood. I couldn't move. 'Soft.' The robot hissed as he trained the laser cannon straight at me, and I saw the trigger lights come on.

It was only a second, but the robot was distracted. The cannon wavered. Then Horatio Dumpty yelled, 'Over here Metal-Head!' and the full power of the water jet caught Hy-Tek in the chest.

With a howl of fury, the great metal bully crashed back.

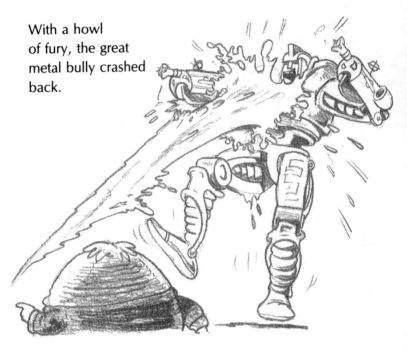

He tried to get up, flailing his arms among the other fallen robots, firing randomly this way and that in his frustration. But now he was down, it was clear that Hy-Tek wasn't getting up again.

He lay there, screeching insanely, with his legs still marching pointlessly on in mid-air, until the water finally seeped into his central cogs, and he ground into silent stillness.

Slowly, we got used to the eerie calm.

One
or two
of us

began to
climb
from
our
hiding
places
and squelch
towards
the

robots.

I stood looking down at the remains of Hy-Tek. He looked smaller now. Just so much scrap, and a few batteries, maybe. Tomorrow all this mess would be cleared away, as if some giant had come along while we slept and put everything in its proper place . . .

It made you kind of wonder what we'd all been so scared of.

CHAPTER TWENTY

I was still standing there after all the others had left.
To be honest I wasn't sure where to go.
The Johnny Nobody case was closed,
the Metalloids wouldn't be
bothering anybody
now. Dumpty, Charley, Ricci,
Miss Teers — they all had
their own lives to go back to.
But what about me? Move on?
Stay? I decided to go back to
the shoebox, hang up my
hat, and sleep. I'd decide the
big questions tomorrow.

I had just stepped over some robot remains when I thought I heard something. I stopped and pricked up my ears.

It was behind me. My hair stood on end. Surely none of these things could still be in working order? There it was again. That noise. It was coming closer . . .

'Fur-ball! What are you doing here?' He made a little whining noise. 'Oh,' I said, 'nowhere else to go, huh? Listen, I'd love to help but I've got worries of my own so – so long.'

Fur-ball didn't move.

'Look,' I pleaded, 'I'm a detective, a drifter travelling down life's dusty highway; a loner, an outsider. How can I be a loner with you chasing my tail the whole time? Now SCOOT!'

I walked again, but I couldn't stop myself listening, to see if I could hear it coming after me. I couldn't. I walked a few more steps. Still no sound. Then I made the fatal mistake. I turned and looked back.

Its funny how things turn out sometimes. I mean if Fur-ball had tried to follow me, I just know I would have chased it away. But it didn't. And *because* it didn't – *because* it just sat and watched, I couldn't leave it. Why? You tell me, I'm just the detective.

'Aw, come on then,' I said. Fur-ball whizzed towards me so fast that for one second I knew how a skittle must feel.

'Fur-ball?' I said, as we walked through the dark back to the shoebox, 'Do you think this could be the start of a beautiful friendship?'

'Yeah. Me too.'

THE END